I0583613

WAITING FOR Someone?

STAN DAVIES

Matchstick Literary
1-888-306-8885
orders@matchliterary.com

INTRODUCTION

During WW2, I lived with my mother, her sister Lena, and my grandparents, Walter and Sarah Owen. The five of us lived in a two-up, two-down cottage on the outer edge of Greater Manchester. I was born on the first of November 1939, just in time to catch the start of the war. My father was called up to the army, and I never saw him again until he was demobbed in 1946. If I had known what was to follow and what my relationship with him would be, I would have been more grateful for those carefree years.

On father's return from Italy and subsequent release from the army, he, mother, and I moved to a similar two-up, two-down a couple of streets away. The second bedroom was unusable due to extreme damp, so we all slept in the same room. I slept in a single bed in the corner, and Mum and Father in a double bed in another corner. When my sister arrived, her cot was next to me.

I was seven years old when we moved to that house, and I was about to learn what marriage was all about in the bedroom. I used to go to bed early in the hope that I would be asleep before they came to bed. Sometimes I was, but most times, I learned the noises and vocabulary of a sexual relationship after a separation of six years.

I have no doubt that my father experienced a multitude of horrors during his service. He served on the front line in Italy, France, and North Africa, and was on board a ship on his way to the Far East when the events at Hiroshima and Nagasaki brought things to an abrupt halt. Perhaps experiencing all the terrible events was what caused him to become the bully and violent man that he was.

When I was eleven years old, we became the proud occupants of a three-bedroom council house, brand-spanking-new and in the very heart of the town. And best of all, I had my own bedroom. My little sister had her own bedroom, also, and was consequently spared the early sex education I endured. The new house was a ten-minute walk from the secondary school that I was about to attend, so that was another plus.

Friday and Saturday nights were my parents' night out at the pubs of Oldham, and I was the unpaid babysitter, I had to be home by seven o'clock on those two nights to safeguard my baby sister so that my parents could hit the town. This began when I was ten, and my sister was six. It continued until I was fifteen. I had to be home by seven, no excuses.

One evening I learned what happens when I failed to be there. I had been playing street football with a couple of friends when I looked at my new watch. I bought it with money from my paper round. I delivered papers in the early mornings and early evenings six days a week for fifteen shillings a week; that's seventy-five pence in today's money. And oh, my God, shock and horror, it was three minutes past seven. It took another three minutes to run home full pelt. I rushed in the back door and went through the kitchen and into the living room.

There stood Father, face like thunder. "You're late!" he roared.

"Not much," I said, glancing at my watch.

The next thing I knew, the back of my head hit the kitchen door. He had punched me full in the face and sent me flying back two metres. As I lay on the living room floor, nose bleeding, I heard him storm out the front door, slamming it behind him.

The longer-term effect of that interlude was profound. I vowed there and then to get away from that man as soon as I was able. I couldn't wait until I was old enough and big enough to even the score.

Now here is a very strange thing. I was sixteen, coming home from work on my bike, and quite literally hit by a bus. I remember nothing of the accident. Apparently I was unconscious and taken by ambulance to the local hospital with severe head injuries. Now, here is the kicker. I was accompanied to the hospital and to theatre by my father, the same man who thought nothing of giving me (and my mother, who had many a face injury having "walked into a door") a backhander for some trivial misdemeanour.

My mother told me that my father pushed me around on the hospital trolley. If anyone else did it, I became agitated and only settled down again when he did it. Amateur psychiatrists, make of that what you like. I only trusted my father when I was unconscious.

CHAPTER 1

Swings and Roundabouts

I was seventeen and unattached, and the fair was in town. The Market Square in Oldham was transformed with dodgem cars and coconut shies. My friend Joe and I jumped on the number 12 bus and headed for the lights and the noise. Oldham Wakes week was the only place to be. Back in the day, every town in Lancashire had a week in early summer when the cotton mills closed their doors, and the better-off workers headed for Blackpool, New Brighton, or Southport to sit on the beach and get sunburned. For those of us who could not afford to get on a charabary (a coach), the fair—or in the local vernacular, the Wakes—was an eagerly anticipated substitute.

It wasn't long before a couple of likely girls caught my eye. One was short and slim, and the other was taller. Both were pretty and, more important, available.

We caught up with them on the merry-go-round. It was nearly impossible to have a conversation with someone going up and down as the girls always seemed to be up when we were down and down when we were up. But there was nothing more innovative than a teenage boy in pursuit of a pretty girl.

We didn't know it then, but this was day 1 of a thirty-five-year relationship.

We arranged to meet the next day and go to the movies. Back then, it was the only way to be with your girlfriend in the dark and close.

Joe and I caught the next bus home; we lived in the same street. It was time to find out who was going to be with whom. Of course, we both fancied the same girl, Irene, so it was agreed we would allow the girls to choose. Whoever went with whomever would be the norm.

I went to bed that night hoping I would be the one for her as Irene was the girl of my dreams.

The next day dawned, and I headed for the bus stop. I checked my reflection in the mirror as I went through the hallway. Hair OK. Sideburns OK. Jeans OK. Cool black shirt OK.

Joe was waiting for me at the bus stop at the end of the street—looking every inch the cool dude he was! *Here we go. Game on!*

We were waiting at the bus stop in the town centre. Finally came a bus crowded with Saturday night revellers. Was she there? No. False alarm. Would they turn up? Had they found someone else?

Then I felt a tap on the shoulder from behind. It was Irene. They had caught an earlier bus! She slipped her arm through mine and asked, "Waiting for someone?"

I caught a glimpse of Joe rolling his eyes with a "just my luck" look.

The friendship became a romance before anyone really noticed. We didn't have any problems that we couldn't deal with.

Joe and Irene's friend after a few months agreed to go their separate ways, while Irene and I were in love for the very first time! We were together almost every day but were never alone enough to take the affair that final step into a full-blown sexual relationship. And as it turned out, that was just as well.

Before meeting Irene, Joe and I had booked and paid for (£22, no less) a holiday to San Sebastian in Spain's Basque region. A further complication was Irene had booked a holiday in Blackpool in Squires Gate Holiday Camp. Spain was two weeks before Blackpool. Problem!

She didn't want me to go. But I had been looking forward to it for months, and anyway, Thomas Cook's office had my money. A refund was not on the table. She offered to cancel her holiday if I did the same. No deal. Big problem. It was our first falling out. It was serious and looked like the romance was over.

I went to Spain. She went to Blackpool, where she met someone, and I was then out of the picture. I was devastated. I tried to contact her, but short of going to her home, that was not possible. (There were no mobile phones in those days.)

My reaction to the split was dramatic, childish, and stupid. But in my defence, I was seventeen years old and had no idea what I was going to do. So I joined the Royal Air Force, the RAF. Yes, I know that was an extreme overreaction, but in my defence, I was—er! I have none. It was plain knee-jerk reaction to a situation out of my control.

CHAPTER 2

Royal Air Force Early Days

I joined the RAF in 1957 and completed my basic training at RAF West Kirkby, near Liverpool. I was then transferred to RAF Compton Basset in the county of Wiltshire for trade training. On completion of the course, I was posted to Bawtry, near Doncaster, where Irene re-entered my life.

I was manning the switchboard when I took a call from the RAF police at the main entrance to the base. The man said, "There is a woman at the main gate asking for you."

Luckily, the duty officer was a member of the same football team as I. Otherwise, the woman asking for me would have needed to find another way to contact me.

After getting my co-worker to cover for me, I headed for the main gate, with no idea who was waiting for me as I had no friends in the village.

To my surprise, it was Irene. She had gotten my address from my mother, taken the train to Doncaster, and then ridden a local bus to the camp. I hadn't seen or heard from her for months, so I was wary of this sudden appearance more than sixty miles from home.

She told me she was booked into the motel in the village and wanted to talk. I was working until six o'clock, so I arranged to meet her at the local pub when I got off shift.

She was "so sorry," she said. The holiday romance at Blackpool meant nothing to her. It was just a reaction to the disappointment of my refusal to change my travel plans. She was desperate to get back together with me. It was the long Easter weekend, so she had three days off work and decided to try to get us back together—if I was willing.

I was totally freaked out by all this. I was angry, surprised, and happy all at the same time when she played her trump card. She had booked us both in to the motel in the hope that I could forget about the past and start a new beginning.

I was eighteen, and she was a virgin (probably). I agreed to stay with her for the long weekend, and then we would see what we could salvage from the situation.

We kissed and made up.

After three days and two nights of sex, laughter, alcohol, and more sex, I was hooked. I agreed to come home to Oldham on my next weekend off. Our romance was on again with a vengeance.

We established a routine for the next few months. When I could, I took a couple of days' leave and went to her, and when I was working, she came to me.

It was wonderful. Absence really does make the heart grow fonder. But, of course, it was too good to last. It all came to an abrupt halt when I was posted not to some sleepy little airfield in Cheshire. Oh no! Too much to ask. Christmas Island was my next destination—twelve thousand miles away. It was so far away and remote that even a letter took more than a week to reach its destination.

Needless to say, we were devastated. The only plus was the posting was for one year. The average overseas posting at that time was two years, such as for Aden, or three years, such as for Singapore, Cyprus, and Malta.

I had a weeklong embarkation leave. We met every day, and there were tears; not all of them were mine! Then I was on my way to London in full dress uniform, kitbag on my shoulder.

Now I must admit, sorry though I was to be leaving Irene and my family (well, my mum and sister), there was a tinge of adventure in the air. We were flying in a four-engine, propeller-driven, chartered aircraft. Our itinerary included a first leg of London to Goose Bay in Canada and then to Vancouver, British Columbia, where we were delayed due to some problem with the aircraft. We stayed two nights and got to see a fair bit of the city.

Our next stop was Honolulu, Hawaii. Then we had a short hop of a couple of hours to Christmas Island.

I think it is public knowledge what was happening on Christmas

Island in the late 1950s, but as a signatory of the Official Secrets Act, I will keep my record of my time there to social and personal events.

First impressions were not good. I saw row on row of tents. The only buildings were made of wood. After spending the last couple days in Canada, being two degrees above the equator was hot and humid. There were two main centres: Main camp, the larger, and HMS Resolution, which was not a ship but a shore base. In navy slang, it was called a stone frigate, although a coral frigate would have been more accurate as I never saw a single stone the whole time I was there.

I shared a four-man tent with three sailors, or "matelots" as they preferred. We got along very well and became good friends. Workwise, I took charge of the telephone switchboard, which was located in a wooden hut on the edge of the lagoon. If the day got too hot, a dip in the ocean was only ten paces away. And a makeshift diving platform had been erected and was in constant use by off-duty sailors.

There was an estimated four thousand people on the island. Air force, army, (Royal Engineers), as well as the navy and Royal Marines.

The only other buildings were the mess hall, the toilets and showers, and the NAAFI. It was the only place I ever saw that had urinals out in the open—just a trough, where the contents ran through a pipe onto the sand below. No cover, no privacy because no women! Not one. So the powers that be saw no point in wasting time and money building closed-in urinals.

The short-sightedness of this approach was highlighted when a carload of females (air hostesses) were being driven round the island by the Padre and were treated to naked sailors urinating in troughs at points around the base.

The orders were posted the following day.

Army: Behaviour contrary to order number 286 has been seen recently.
Any further instances will be punishable by fines or detention.
Navy: The boastful display of bollocks is to cease forthwith!

I think the air hostesses rather enjoyed it.

Meanwhile, Irene and I continued our relationship by post. Two letters per week each was the norm, plus the occasional photograph, some of which I still have.

I counted the days to my return to the real world as the days in my surreal world slipped by.

Some people would probably think what I complained about while living on a Pacific island with sun, sea, and sand sounded a bit like paradise. But the reality was boredom. There were no TV, cinemas, shops, libraries, restaurants, or women. Anyone who fancies it should try living in a tent for a year with no running water or electricity in the sleeping accommodation. The only connection with the real world was Radio Honolulu, whose main effect on us was pointing out what we were missing.

As the months slowly crept by, and I reached better than half way—that is, I had fewer months to go than I had already done—I was counting weeks, not months.

When I had six weeks left to do, my world was once again turned upside down; I didn't get a letter from Irene for a couple of weeks. This was odd, as previously, I received two per week, almost without fail, for the last ten and a half months. Regular and much looked forward to.

In the last letter that I had written to her, I told her how much I missed her and had gone a little bit over the top for my homecoming, even suggesting getting married. I hoped to surprise her with the amount of money I had saved as there were no shops to spend our wages, except the NAAFI, and that was almost all on food and drink.

Mail was eagerly looked forward to and was a major morale booster. All except for one one kind of letter, the dreaded "Dear John," so called because when things were going well, letters from wives and girlfriends invariably began, "My darling," or, "My dearest," or similar endearments, but if the marriage or relationship was in trouble, the letter almost without fail began, "Dear John," or Dave, or in my case, "Dear Stan." She was sorry, but she had to tell me that she was breaking up with me. There was no one else. It was just that because of the long separation, she had come to realise she didn't love me anymore.

I was angry and bitterly disappointed. It was frustrating being so far away. I felt sure if I could just see her, all would be well again. Suddenly, six weeks to go seemed like an eternity.

If I had known then what I know now, I don't think I would be able to control my actions when I returned to the United Kingdom six weeks and two days later.

CHAPTER 3

New York, New York: So Good, They Named It Twice

I was in New York, walking down Times Square, having arrived there from Honolulu and Los Angeles, and staying in the Governor Clinton Hotel. I wore full dress uniform, which felt a bit strange after a year just wearing KD (Khaki Drill) shorts and short-sleeve shirts. However, the magic of the uniform was working if the invitations for drinks from women of that fine city were to be believed.

In a couple of days, I was back in Mum and Dad's place in Oldham on six weeks' disembarkation leave, awaiting my next posting

Irene, meanwhile, was nowhere to be seen. She had apparently rented a small apartment with a female friend somewhere in the town, but my parents had not seen her since Christmas, and it was now June. Irene had come to my parents' house at Christmas with gifts for my sister, Pam, and invited to stay to lunch.

Now, Irene did not drink alcohol except at weddings and funerals. But as it was Christmas, there was beer and wine served with the food, and she had a little too much of the sweet white wine. After the meal, she was feeling a bit unwell, and someone suggested a walk in the fresh air. Mum was doing the washing up, so father volunteered to go with her as she was a bit unsteady on her feet. So Father and Irene went for the walk.

The back of the house overlooked a laneway and a plot of shoreland which contained a relic from the war, an air raid shelter. There were no windows or doors. Just four quite small rooms connected by a long narrow corridor. As kids, we used to play in there if it was raining, but it was dark and smelly.

The kitchen window directly overlooked the building. My mother was in the kitchen, washing dishes, and had a clear view of the shelter. What she saw that day she never told me until thirty-five years later. And when she did, I understood why she had kept quiet about it.

She said Father and Irene were in the entrance to the air raid shelter, Irene up against the wall and Father with his back to the window from where Mum watched. But importantly, Irene knew that she could be seen. Irene's dress was lifted, and her underwear was around one ankle. Mum said she could not tell from the kitchen whether Irene was a willing participant or a victim. On being pressed, she said that Irene did seem to be "agitated"—her word.

A few minutes later, Father returned to the house alone. When Mum asked him where Irene was, he said she had a bus to catch.

That was the last time they saw her, but she did send my sister a birthday card in March. And, of course, she was still writing to me and continued to do so after Christmas for another six months. It was only when my return home was imminent that the "Dear Stan" letter arrived. Time to return home.

CHAPTER 4

Back to Civilisation.

I soon got back into the daily routine, looking up Joe for a chat and going to the football at Boundary Park, the home of the local team, Oldham Athletic. I was getting a bit bored. Oldham is a lively little town, but New York it is not.

I decided to go to the Friday night dance in the town centre, half hoping Irene would be there, and half not giving a damn if she wasn't.

She wasn't!

But a dear friend of hers was. And unknown to me, she was in the telephone kiosk near the entrance, ringing Irene to give her the news. Twenty minutes later, Irene walked into the dance hall, which by now was bursting at the seams with people with dancers bumping into each other. I did not see her at first in the crowd, but it soon became obvious that something was going on in one corner of the floor.

These were the days when jive was king. Or in Irene's case, queen. Boy, could she jive. She was dancing with her friend, and they had quite an audience. Irene was a great dancer, and jive was her specialty. She was generally quite a shy person, not given to displays of any kind, but with Elvis on the radio, she could really fly, spinning and ducking and diving like there was no tomorrow.

Needless to say, she ignored me. She told me later she was waiting for me to approach her. My view was, as the injured party, it was up to her to speak to me. I know this all sounds pathetic, but we had reached an impasse about who was going to blink first.

I was saved by the band. The next dance was to be an "Excuse me."

If someone you fancied was dancing with a partner, you could tap the partner on the shoulder say, "Excuse me," and that person had to retire. You then danced with the remaining partner. I don't know who invented that routine, but whoever you are, "Thank you." I owe you one!

The ice was broken, and when the dance ended, we sat down together and talked. We dodged around the main topic for a while, just the, "How are you?" "Fine." "Oh, that's good." Then inevitably I asked, "What happened? The hard part was nearly over. What brought about your change of heart?"

Remember at this time I had no knowledge of the events of Christmas. As far as I knew, everything had been fine, and then, for no obvious reason, it was not.

We sat and talked and continued to dodge the main problem. But I still loved her and could not get a convincing answer as to why she broke up with me.

We compromised and agreed to meet at the cinema the next day.

CHAPTER 5

Early Days.

We met outside the Odeon Cinema the next afternoon. But since it was a lovely, sunny, summer's day, we elected to go to the park instead. We sat on a park bench by the boating lake and talked and talked and talked.

There were no easy solutions, but the overwhelming feeling was we wanted to be together. It became obvious that we still loved each other. And that, in the end, was all that truly mattered.

In retrospect, it is obvious that she did not know if I knew about the events of Christmas. In fact, I would not know until my mother told me all those years later. (I owe my mum a big thank you for all those years.) We were back together, and this time it had to be permanent or not at all. No hangovers from the past. We decided to get married.

Now I don't know who made up these rules, but they were like this. As a serving member of the armed forces, I had to ask permission to marry from the powers that be. And being under the age of twenty-one, I also had to get permission from my parents, as did Irene.

The powers that be of the RAF granted permission, as did Irene's parents. But only one of my parents agreed. No prizes for guessing which one did not. Permission denied. Father refused permission, so what now? No reason was given, just a flat no.

According to the law of England, I could fight for my country, but unless my daddy said so, I could not marry the woman I loved. Whoever said, "The law is an ass," knew their business.

Where to now? I had a month of disembarkation leave left to find out.

CHAPTER 6

Eloped to Scotland.

As a child, Irene and her brother, Peter, spent some time living in Scotland after her mother and father divorced. Her stepfather was Scottish, and after her mother died, and Irene, Peter, and stepfather lived in Scotland with his parents. So far as we knew, the stepfather and step-grandparents still lived in Scotland. The age of consent for marriage north of the border was eighteen, which is why Gretna Green was so popular with runaways. So it was grandparents, here we come.

The rule was we had to establish residence for three weeks, and then we could marry in a registry office. I had four weeks of leave left, so there was no time to lose. I was staying at my parents' house, so I had to come up with why I was leaving early. I told them I had been re-called early to fill a position which had just become vacant. Irene told her parents the truth. We caught the train from Manchester to Glasgow, and then on to Kirkonnel by bus.

To say the step-grandparents were surprised to see us was a bit of an understatement. They had not seen Irene for some years as her stepfather (their son) had contracted some illness which prevented him from caring for them. Peter and Irene were taken into care back in England some years ago.

To their everlasting credit, Irene's step-grandparents welcomed us into their home and backed us all the way. Without their aid and support, we could never have achieved what we did.

It was important that we go to the registrar's office and fill in the intention to marry paperwork. This we did next day. The only question the registrar asked us was, "Do your parents know what you intend to do?" I thought for a moment he was going to refuse us, but we told the truth and said no. He said the reason he asked was if anyone contacted his office asking about us and our intentions, he would say he never heard of us!

Thank you, unknown official. Three weeks duly passed, and we had to endure sleeping separately, Irene in the spare room, and me on the sofa in the living room. The elderly couple was old school, and we were so grateful for their help and support that we were happy to obey the house rules.

The time duly passed, and on the appointed day, we became Mr and Mrs Davies. The rules stated there were to be two witnesses to the ceremony. Irene's aunt was one, and the registrar once again came to our aid, designating his clerk as the second one.

To cap a very special day, when we returned to the house, there was lunch and a wonderful wedding cake. A group of family and friends were there to put the finishing touches on what was probably at that time the best day of my life.

The final gesture from these wonderful people was from Irene's aunt, who lived a few miles away in the beautiful Scottish countryside. She invited us to stay with her for a couple days' honeymoon. Needless to say, we accepted as the final touch to a perfect day, one that we would never forget.

But time was catching up with us, and my leave was nearly over. We had to get home to face the music and find out where my next posting was.

Back at my parents' house, my mother and sister were home. Father was still at work or on his way home. The tension in the house was palpable. The clock chimed five o'clock, and Father was due any minute. Finally, I heard his key in the front door lock, and he walked into the room.

He looked at Irene with some surprise and then at me. The time to stand up to the bully had arrived. I was not a cowering eight-year-old or even a fifteen-year-old babysitter anymore. I was twenty years old and extremely fit and hardened by two years of military service. And I was now bigger than him. Nevertheless, it was a situation where one false word or move could have been catastrophic.

He took off his hat, looked hard at me, and asked "So are you married or what?"

The temptation to say, "Or what," was almost too much. But I struggled to come up with, "We're married."

It turned out that my mum had written to me at the base where I had told them I was going. When it was returned marked, "Not at this address," they knew something was going on.

We left the house, and I had to get to my new post—Norfolk.

Irene still had her flat with her friend. The separation was not for long. After a couple weeks in Norfolk, I was able to rent a caravan in a park a few hundred yards from the camp. Irene joined me as soon as she could.

A Son is born.

We were married on March 4,1960. Our son, Nicholas, was born December 18. The same year. He was born at the RAF hospital in the county of the isle of Ely, the smallest county in Britain at the time. It has since been joined to Cambridgeshire and is no longer an independent county.

Irene was taken by ambulance to hospital as I was going to work at the telephone exchange at the base of RAF Watton in Norfolk. At about 7:30 p.m., I received a phone call to tell me that I was the proud father of a healthy baby girl. No sooner had I digested this information than I received another phone call to tell me that my wife had given birth to a son. "What, twins?"

"No, no. Sorry, the first call was a false alarm and concerned a Mrs Davison."

"You are sure now it is only one baby."

"Most definitely!"

"Thank you for clearing that up." I was a dad. Hooray!

Irene was released from hospital on Christmas Eve, after six days, which was a little sooner than usual so the two of them could be home for Christmas. Unfortunately, I couldn't join them for long as I was working Christmas Day for the third year in a row. I didn't know what I had to do to get a Christmas off.

Nick was a good baby. He loved attention, and he really loved food. Only milk at first, of course, but he was on to solids in no time and devoured practically any kind of food we gave him.

CHAPTER 8

More Training

After three or four months, I was chosen to go back to Wiltshire for a Morse code course, which was to last five months. So it was pack our bags and off to Wiltshire and the local caravan site. It was quite a way from the base, but fortunately, the RAF provided a bus as there were quite a few RAF families living there.

It was in the village of Avebury, famous for its prehistoric stone circles. Many experts thought it a more important site than Stonehenge, which was better known but nowhere near as big or as old as Avebury.

I was quite surprised to be on a wireless operator course as Watton was an air base with runways and aircraft, a proper air force posting. What was I going to do with my newly acquired Morse code skills? Wiltshire was an interesting experience, learning new skills and meeting new people. The question of why I needed to learn Morse code skills was eventually answered.

After returning from the course, I settled back into the routine as before.

CHAPTER 9

With another Family member.

Nick was growing up, almost three years old. We were thinking about if not school, perhaps kindergarten, when I was told to prepare in the near future for a posting to Cyprus. It would be for three years, taking me almost to the end of my nine-year term in the RAF.

Irene was pregnant. The baby was due late February or early March. Depending on when I had to take up my new post, whether we could travel together was a concern. I discussed it with my senior officer and was assured that the transfer was not imminent; the person I was to replace was not scheduled to leave until June and, in the event, did not leave until late July.

Marcelle was born on 5 March at my aunt's—Aunty Lena, my mother's younger sister—house as my parents had moved to another house on the same street as the old one, but it had only two bedrooms, one for my parents, and one for my sister. There was no room for me or my growing family. Also, of course, it gave my father a perfect excuse for getting rid of me, so I could not visit when I was on leave.

Aunty Lena's house had two bedrooms, and arrangements were made for Irene to move there when the birth was due. I don't think Aunty Lena was thrilled by the idea—or Irene either—but it was better than having the baby alone or among strangers if I was in Cyprus and she in England. Irene and Nick moved up to my aunt's house in late February, and I moved on to the base. There was still no firm date for the transfer to Cyprus.

I was given emergency leave to travel up to Oldham and be present at the birth, which was upon us almost at once. It was as though the baby was as anxious to be born and off to the Mediterranean as we were.

On my second night with Irene, I was woken just after midnight as she was having contractions. We had a phone number to ring for the midwife, which would have been really convenient if we had a phone! However, there was a telephone kiosk in the next street. I quickly dressed and went to make the call.

The midwife was with us within the hour. She quickly examined Irene and asked her a few questions after which she asked me, "Where is the telephone." I pointed it out as it was visible from the upstairs bedroom window. She quickly scribbled a number on a note pad and told me to ring the doctor; she thought there may be need of him. She assured me that everything was under control and not to worry. She was just being extra cautious.

I rang the doctor. His practice was only in the next street, but I had no idea where he lived. And it was highly unlikely that he would be at his place of work at three in the morning.

He duly arrived, and I asked him if there was a problem. He assured me that if so, he would call an ambulance and take Irene to the local hospital. He told me to follow him and went up the stairs. He had a close look at Irene and spoke to the midwife.

He turned to me and said, "I think we will be able to handle this. The umbilical cord is around the baby's neck, and it is being held back. I am going to try to free it. Please feel free to stay with us as an observer and if we need you to assist."

The doctor put on his rubber gloves and started to try to turn the baby's head, the top of which was just visible. After a few seconds, he hooked his finger round the cord and freed it. The result was immediate, and the rest of the baby's head appeared. The midwife put her hand at the back of my head and pushed it down towards the baby. "There, look. We have a baby." And with a rush and a slippery sound, like a cork coming out of a bottle, we did, a beautiful little girl doing what she did so well for the early part of her babyhood, crying loud and clear. I loved her then, and I love her still.

CHAPTER 10

Back to Work.

With dawn just rising on the horizon, mother and baby were doing fine. Our family was complete, and so it was to prove for many years to come.

I returned to base to find we had been given a date for our departure. It was in some four months' time, so there was no need to rush.

However, Aunty Lena, being the miserable old spinster that she was, wanted us out of the way, so she could go back to her narrow existence without delay. Fortunately, our old caravan back near the camp was still vacant, and I was able to negotiate a short-term rental. The van's owner thought a short-term rental was preferable to no rental at all.

So we reunited as a family. Irene later told me that she was grateful for the chance to have her baby there, but she was sorry to have to tell me that Aunty Lena was the most miserable, disagreeable person it had ever been her misfortune to meet.

CHAPTER 11

Cyprus.

We left for Cyprus some three months later, in late July. We flew in the latest jet passenger liner, a Comet 4B. It was the epitome of air travel at the time, the fastest and most comfortable aircraft in the world.

Marcelle cried the whole way, six hours nonstop. The air hosts and hostesses tried everything they knew. They even got the co-pilot out of the cockpit to try his baby-soothing skills, but to no avail.

We could not understand why she would not stop crying. We think it was something to do with air pressure in her ears as the cabin was, of course, pressurised. When we landed and the doors were opened, she stopped crying immediately and slept for four hours.

We overnighted in a hotel in Nicosia, the capital, and left the next morning for Famagusta, which was where our house was. I had no idea what to expect regarding the house. The only thing I knew about it was that it was not a "married quarter" but a private house on long-term rental to the air force.

Famagusta is on the south-east of the island. Its population consisted mainly of Greek-speaking ethnic residents but with a significant number of Turkish-speaking people who mostly lived in the "old city," a quaint walled city on the outskirts of the main town.

Our new home was in a cul-de-sac, so there was no through traffic. It was in a Turkish area outside the old city. It consisted of a block of four apartments, and two detached houses. The Turkish owners lived in one of the apartments on the top floor. Their family was two adults, two teenage boys, and a grandma, who lived on the flat roof of the apartments. Yes, really on the roof.

Our house was across the street from the apartments. All the rest of the accommodations were occupied by RAF personnel. It was a private, cosy little community we were destined to come to love.

We were picked up from the airport hotel by a RAF driver, who took us to the house. It was about an hour drive, and we had time to question the driver. It turned out he lived in the other house in the street, the one directly across from us.

He was from Wales, so we call him Taf. We became good friends as we did with all the residents at that street. Taf told us that the airman who was the corporal on my shift lived in the other top-floor apartment. He was to be my boss and bosom buddy on the football field. We will call him Jack as he was Cornish.

We duly arrived at what was to be our home for the next three years. It was well above our expectations after years of living in rented caravans and before that, military bases and for me, a year in a tent. And for Irene, children's homes and cheap apartments.

It was a single-storey brick house with a garden and a garage, though I had no car (soon to be remedied). There were three bedrooms, two bathrooms, and a great kitchen. And it was fully furnished, down to the egg cups and ashtrays. It was everything we could wish for.

We had a few days to settle in and find our bearings. Then I had to go to work. There was a bus to the base, which I could catch at the end of the street. And as Jack was on the same shift, I could catch a lift with him.

One thing quickly became obvious; I was going to need a car and some driving lessons if I wanted to find my way to the shops, the beach, or to enjoy any of the facilities. Local bus service was non-existent; people had to drive or take a taxi.

The work shift at the base was a four-watch system, A, B, C, and D. I was on B watch, but each watch had its own staff and NCOs. The first day was 7:00 p.m. to midnight; day 2, 12:30 p.m. to 7:00 p.m. Day 3 was 6:00 a.m. to 12:30 p.m., and day 4 was the midnight to 6:00 a.m. shift, known as the doggo for reasons unknown. Then came the best part–two days off. This was the pattern of shifts I worked for the three years I was there.

CHAPTER 12

Learning to drive.

The family was all settled in our new environment. The weather was all that we could expect. Sunshine every day and pleasantly cool evenings enabled Irene and me to sit on the veranda at the front of the house with a glass of wine or, more often, a coffee. Taf and his wife lived directly opposite us, doing the same thing, enjoying the star-spangled sky and the cooling breeze after the heat of the day.

Taf was a qualified motor mechanic as well as his driving duties. He offered to give me some driving lessons when he finished renovating an old vehicle that he was working on in his spare time. There was a flat, open area near the end of the street, with a grove of orange trees on two sides of it. And as mentioned, the street was a cul-de-sac, so there was no traffic to worry about.

Taf finished his work on the old, open, two-seater car, and we were ready to go. After explaining what the controls were for and which control did what, we were off on the football pitch–size open ground behind our house.

The old car was a manual three-speed car. But Taf had it going in top condition, and my driving improved daily.

Came the day when Taf thought I was ready to take my driving test. So I filled in the forms, and it was set for a few days' time.

Now, in all the excitement of getting myself ready, there was an element that we had not realised. When I took the test, it was in the streets of Famagusta, a Greek town, where all the road signs were naturally in Greek, of which I knew nothing, and Turkish, of which I knew even less. In the end. it was my lack of Turkish language skills that failed me. I now know the word *stomata* is Turkish for stop, so I failed my driving test because I failed to stop at a stomata sign. It was a bit lucky there was not much traffic about at the time.

I passed at the second try. So let's go and buy a car. It was a bright red Austin Mini with an 800cc engine and in lovely condition. Having the car meant the family could go to the beach or shops whenever we liked. We could explore our surroundings. The old city was particularly attractive and only a five-minute drive away.

The Turkish family who lived opposite and owned the apartments had a shop in the old city. We were keen to explore it as they had told us of the history and facilities it contained. One of the facilities in the old city was an excellent football (soccer) stadium.

CHAPTER 13

Football Failure.

Now Jack was a very good footballer and had been signed to Chelsea football club in the English first division as a young man. He did not make the grade with Chelsea, but he was selected to represent the RAF against the army and navy, and was still the best player I ever played with. A cut above the rest of us.

He was invited by the local football club to play for them in a friendly against a touring Turkish team in the old city stadium. He asked me if I would join him, and I jumped at the chance to play at that level. Previously, I only played at the amateur level. The game was to be refereed by an army officer of Jacks acquaintance, who was the best qualified official on the island.

The game was a big deal for the locals, and there was a decent crowd in attendance. Unfortunately, the local players seemed to think the only way to victory was to kick the towners off the field, and the ref was kept very busy.

First one and then another were sent off from the home team. That only seemed to make things worse, so inevitably, the ref blew his whistle, said the game was abandoned, and left the stadium in a huff. We were never asked to play again!

CHAPTER 14

Childhood Woes

After several uneventful months, we were well and truly in the swing of things, finding our way around the island and discovering new beaches and places of interest.

One day I brought an English-language newspaper home. A new arrival to our watch had brought it with him and was about to throw it in the bin. I asked him to give it to me as we missed the morning paper that had been an everyday thing back in Britain.

The main story was about some well-known man being charged for sexually assaulting young boys. The newspaper lay about the house for some days. Then one day, we were having a tidy-up day, and as I was about to put it in the bin, Irene out of the blue said, "Peter and I were sexually assaulted when we were kids." I was shocked and asked by who.

"Our stepfather. After Mother died, he used to give us money to masturbate him a couple of times a week."

I asked her if she told anyone. She said she had not as he had told them "bad things" would happen if they did. Irene was seven years old and Peter was nine at the time. I wondered if the reason they were shunted off to the orphanage had anything to do with that.

One day the Turkish boy from across the road was out in front of our house, talking to Nick and giving him a push on his tricycle. He often came across for a chat. He had very good English skills and was a polite and agreeable youngster.

If his grandma was on her rooftop lookout post, she often shouted down to him. One day I asked him what she was saying, and he laughed and said, "She is telling me not to eat any pig." It didn't work as he was quite fond of the odd bacon sandwich. But he never admitted it to the old woman.

This young man was spending more and more time at our place. The kids loved him coming over and talking to them, and his English skills also improved by the day.

We got into the habit of inviting one or two of my workmates to spend the weekend with us to give them a break from the camp and to sample some home cooking for a change. The ones who came appreciated the chance to get away from the strict rules and regulations of the base.

We had plenty of room to sleep a couple of guys. And one day we had one of my football mates, a Scot called Jock! What else?

I was on the morning shift, 6:00 a.m. to 12:30 p.m., so I caught the shift bus at 5:40 a.m. I arrived home around 2:00 p.m., Jock met me on the front veranda and asked, "Have you got a minute before you go in?"

I said OK, and we sat on the wall outside the house. He had been in the shower about ten this morning and had left his towel in the spare room. He just draped the bathroom towel around him as he nipped out to retrieve his own when he literally bumped into the teenager from across the road coming out of the kids' bedroom, with Irene close behind.

He said they both looked very surprised to see him as the shower was still running, which could be clearly heard by all parties. From their reactions, it was clear they thought he was still in there. Jock apologised for his garb and went back into the bathroom.

He said he loved staying with us and thought about keeping quiet. But as a fair, churchgoing man, he felt he had to tell me what he had seen.

It was damning evidence of something going on, but hearsay! Could I accuse them of having an affair or even spur of the moment sex? It would be Irene's word against Jock's, and I was a bit inclined to believe her, although what Jock had to gain from the incident was minimal. He was never invited to stay with us after that, which was a shame, As things turned out, he was 100 percent correct.

Wrongly, I decided not to challenge her with any misconduct as it would always be her word against Jocks and no way to prove either way. I decided to let it go but to be more watchful in future.

A few weeks later I came home from a night shift at about 6:50 a.m. to find Irene out of bed and looking very pale. I asked her what was going on, and she told me she had a miscarriage in the early hours of the morning. She awoke when feeling discomfort, which built to real pain. And when she went to the toilet, the foetus, showing no sign of life, fell into the toilet as she sat on it.

I asked her where it was, and she said she flushed it away. That seemed a bit radical, but she said it was a spur of the moment thing. She could not bear to examine the foetus and wanted rid of it.

I said I thought she should see a doctor as there was a military hospital a few miles up the road, but she said no. She said she would be OK with a few hours' sleep, and so it proved to be. She slept for four hours, and when she woke up, she was more composed, and looked and sounded much better.

Weeks turned into months, and we were living the good life, until one day I collected the mail from the base. Mail was not delivered to the door; I had to collect it from the work. There was a letter for Irene from one of the London areas. One of the guys who spent some weekends with us lived in Hampstead, and he had recently finished his tour of duty when I got home. I told Irene there was a letter for her postmarked Hampstead Heath, and the only person I knew who lived there was Harry J., and I wondered what he wanted.

She opened the letter, and folded into the pages was a ten-pound note. Having read the letter, Irene put it and the bank note back in the envelope and put it in her handbag.

"Can I read it?" I asked. She was very reluctant, but in the end, she said OK, but I could see she was not happy about it.

It was quite a short letter but very interesting. He asked Irene to get him some pills from the chemist for terminating a pregnancy. They were not available in Britain but were quite legal and easy to buy in Cyprus. He enclosed his address and thanked her in advance, saying please return them ASAP, as his girlfriend in Hampstead was a few weeks pregnant.

Very interesting. Why did he ask Irene and not me? I wondered, *He is my friend, after all. And more to the point, how did he know that Irene knew what the pills were and where to get them?*

Now, putting two and two together can often come to five, but Irene's response to these questions was that Tafs wife had told her in passing one day about the pills and their availability. It was not possible to check this as Taf and his wife had returned to Wales a few weeks ago.

I was not convinced, especially with the recent events in our relationship and the amount of time the teenager from the apartments was spending at our place when I was at work. I told her that I did not believe her and that those pills were the cause of her miscarriage. And why on earth would she want to terminate a pregnancy when we had two beautiful children, and another one would have been welcome?

She denied taking the pills. But she had given birth to two healthy babies with no major complications, so why was this one any different.

We had a normal sex life for two people in their mid-twenties. Why would she want to terminate this baby? My theory was that if she was having sex with the kid across the road, who was of Middle Eastern appearance—with jet-black hair and an Asian skin colour—not exactly brown, but not the lily-white and blonde hair that Irene had or the light brown hair and pale skin that was my heritage. What then?

If I was the father, no problem. But if he was, what then? She had no way of knowing who the father was, and she could not risk it and had to terminate.

In a weird sort of way, I felt sorry for her and the mess she had got herself into. But the overwhelming emotion was anger. How could she? Why would she? She knew that she was risking being put on the next aircraft back to the United Kingdom. Not the children, just her. That would have broken her heart; she loved those children. It was an amazingly foolish and thoughtless action, and the next step in this debacle was up to me.

I agonized over it for several days. I was hurt, devastated, undecided. Was it a legacy of her poor treatment during her childhood, the orphanage, her stepfather's antics? I did not yet know about the Christmas thing and my father, so I didn't include that. But she did, and how many things had she endured in the first ten or twelve years of her life, before being rescued on the streets of Oldham by her older brother, Brian, her father, and stepmother?

Irene's older brother, Brian, stayed with his father when their parents divorced, and Irene and Peter went with their mother to Scotland. Brian had been in the market in Oldham and recognised Peter. He asked him his name to be sure, and it was confirmed.

I don't know the details as Irene was reluctant to talk about it, but the result of the brothers meeting was that their stepmother, who was a school mistress and in my book one of the "good guys," insisted that her husband take Peter and Irene out of the orphanage and into their care. They had a young child of three and a big enough house to accommodate the reunited family. For the first time in her life, Irene was in a secure, stable family environment with two brothers and parents who loved and cared for her.

As I said, I knew very little of those early days as Irene was seventeen and sharing an apartment when we met. In spite of the care and attention the three children got. Brian joined the army as soon as he was old enough, Peter joined the air force at a similar young age, and Irene left home at seventeen to live with her school friend, which is where she was when we met. In my uneducated way and given my experience, I knew why young people left home and couldn't wait to get out in the wide world.

So all these thoughts were spinning around in my head. Irene had it tough for a number of formative years, and who was I to judge? Besides, I did not want to make a formal complaint as it did not look well on me, either, as I had turned a blind eye to events that I really should not have. If I had intervened at the start, none of this would have happened, so I was not free from blame.

As so often happens, the problem was solved for me by events in the world. Or at least on the island of Cyprus.

For a number of years, a Greek Cypriot terrorist group, known as EOKA, had caused trouble on the island. They planted bombs and caused fear and disruption around the island as they called for Greek independence. Yhe Turkish minority were getting very concerned by the increase in violence. with shots fired and explosives detonated in Turkish areas.

I was coming home from an evening shift after midnight, and as I came down the street, I saw the lights were on in the house. That was unusual at this late hour. I let myself in the house, and Irene and the children were still up. Irene said, "Thank God you're home. We have had a terrifying few hours." Unknown to us, local Turks had established a machine gun post behind the back, six-foot tall, brick wall. They exchanged fire with unknown assailants on the other side, on open ground, about two hundred yards away.

Irene took me into the kids' bedroom, and there were bullets embedded in the wall and the wooden shutters. That was why she and the children were in the lounge room at the front of the house.

As soon as I was able, I reported the situation to the military police at the base, and they said they would send somebody to assess the situation. A flight sergeant duly arrived, and I showed him the sandbagged, gun emplacement behind our garage. I then showed him the bullets embedded in the walls of the house and the bullet holes in the wooden shutters in the children's bedroom.

That was enough for him. He said we could no longer stay in this house as it was obviously not a safe place any more. He called up another vehicle for our belongings, and we were relocated to a house in central Famagusta, in the Greek part of the town.

The new accommodation was not so big as our previous home, and it did not have much of a garden or a garage, just a parking space for the car. However, it was walking distance from the beach and the local shops, and as I later discovered one of my workmates lived on the same street. We soon settled into the new house, and though we never made friends with the neighbours the way we had in our previous home, especially in the case of a certain young man of Turkish origin, that was a major plus.

Our next-door neighbours were a young couple with a small child. They were Greeks and did not know much English. But they were friendly enough. When they asked about our children, they were delighted to find that Nicholas was our son's name. The lady of the house clapped and said, "Ah, Nickolagi. Very good Greek boy."

It was soon after this move that I was promoted to corporal and put in charge of C watch, which altered my days off but was basically the same system. Nick started school and caught the school bus to Four Mile Point which was run by the British army.

Tension in the town was high as Turkey got involved in the dispute between Greek and Turkish Cypriots and were threatening to commit troops unless the Cypriot government did something about the EOKA situation. One of the airmen on my new shift lived on the same street. His nickname was Icky. Being on the same roster, we were able to carpool, taking turns driving to and from work. Because of the tension on the island, local police put up roadblocks at strategic points. Stopping and searching vehicles added travel time to and from work. It was not unusual to have the car searched two or three times going to and from work. And as the new house was farther away by a couple of miles, the daily commute was a pain; it took up to half an hour longer than before the unrest started.

It was 1966, and England was in the World Cup final. Naturally, the game was on television. Unfortunately, we did not own one, so we were reduced to listening to the match on the British Forces radio broadcast. Or so we thought. The Greek family next door invited me to watch it on their newly acquired TV.

England were playing Germany, and for different reasons, we both wanted England to win, which they duly did. My neighbour and I celebrated the victory with a bottle of ouzo, which went down very nicely. Of course, the commentary was in Greek, but England was the best team in the world—at least until the next World Cup.

On the subject of football, the team I captained at the base had just won the competition for the first time in years, and we were about to celebrate with a party at the base. There were only five teams in the league, but the camp was intense. Our team manager was the watch warrant officer. He had never won it before, so he was a very happy man!

The main thing that I remember of the presentation of the trophy was when the commanding officer's wife presented it to me. I dropped it. A voice from the crowd at the bar said, "How, how, he's dropped it," followed by a rejoinder from the team boss, "But we didn't drop any points." And it was true. We won every game, and so far as anyone could remember, that had never been done before.

Our time in Cyprus was coming to an end. We were due to return to the United Kingdom in the next couple of months, when I would have to decide whether to sign on for a further term in the RAF or to try my luck in the real world. If I chose to extend my stay in the RAF, the minimum time I could sign on for was five years and the maximum to when I was age fifty-five. In other words, a lifetime commitment.

It was not an easy decision as the nature of my position was such that there would only ever be three postings: the one I was in now, the one I left to come here, and Germany. It was the nature of my job and training, and there were no other options. So the decision was to spend the next thirty to thirty-five years as an airman, being shuttled around the world, or sign on for five more years and defer the decision. That last option was something of a cop-out.

My children were nearly six and three. Was I about to burden them with having to change schools every three years? Nick had already been to two schools and was not yet six years old. And after three years of living in a "proper" house, I did not fancy going back to the semi-nomadic life of caravans and temporary accommodations.

I pondered this problem coming home from work in Icky's car. When he dropped me off at my front door, I recognised a bike leaning against the fence. Last seen ridden by the afore-mentioned Turkish teenager.

I let myself in, and there he was, sitting at the kitchen table, drinking a cup of coffee.

Irene was standing by the window, from where she would have seen my arrival. She said, "As you can see, we have a visitor."

I nodded in his direction and, pointing to the back garden, said to Irene, "Irene, a word." We went out the back door and closed it behind us.

I could hardly contain my rage. I could not believe what was going on. But before I could form the words that were spinning around my head, she told me she had no idea what he was doing there; he just turned up out of the blue. I asked her how he knew where we were. And did he know the danger he was in as a Turk in the middle of a Greek town? She denied any involvement in his arrival and seemed just as baffled by his presence as I was.

I returned to the kitchen and told him he had better leave, partly because this was a staunchly Greek area. And partly because if he did not leave, I would call the police.

He looked a bit anxious, as if the penny had just dropped that he had placed himself in danger. I escorted him to the door, and as he left, I told him that if he ever came there again, or tried to contact Irene in any way, he would be in big trouble. He left in a hurry!

I would like to think that was the end of this episode, but there was one final event in the years to come. Even I had to agree the boy did not know how to quit.

After he left, I asked Irene if she really expected me to believe that she had not told him where we were. How else could he find out? It's not that our address was in the phone book.

She reverted to her standard attitude when under pressure; she gave me the "silent treatment" for the next few days. I was busy at work as my time there was running out. I had made up my mind about what I was going to do about my—and her—future. I was going to leave the service and try my luck in "Curvy Street."

We returned to Britain, and I had to report to RAF Gloucester to hand in my uniform and go through the motions of separation. It was not absolute as I had to do three years in the reserve, which meant in the event of another major war, I would be called back to service first, before a general call up.

I remember my father's response when he left the army after WW2. He was told he was in the reserves and could be re-enlisted on very short notice. He returned the form they sent him with the words, "Not interested," scrawled across it. He eventually got a reply, which stated that in the event of a re-enlistment refusal in the future, he would be arrested and imprisoned. So if ever WW3 broke out, Father would be AWOL (absent without leave) and on the run from day 1. Typical!

Irene and the children were back at Aunty Lena's place until I returned. But we soon bought a terraced house in the town, two up two down—two bedrooms and a kitchen and living room. We had a small paved backyard, which was where the toilet was. It was on the same street as the children's primary school, which was convenient. But the main thing about it was that it cost 400 pounds. We paid 200 pounds up front and had a bank loan for the balance. We both soon got employment at a local electronics factory making light bulbs, Irene on the production line and me as a junior foreman.

It was not too taxing, but the hours were 8:00 a.m. until 5:30 p.m. Monday to Friday, and for me, Saturdays from 8:00 a.m. to midday. This was when most of the paperwork for the week was processed, plus any repairs to the machinery was done. It was not rocket science, but it paid the bills, as they say!

At first, it felt a bit strange that both of us worked in the same place, but we soon got used to it. It had the advantage that we could travel to work together in our dark blue Ford Escort.

Another advantage of both of us working in the same building was I could keep an eye out for any work friendships becoming more than just casual acquaintances. There were still things in the past that were unexplained, but with no actual proof and nobody caught in the act or admitting to any indiscretions, we soon settled into a routine. The children were doing well at school. My mother picked them up and stayed with them until we got home from work.

Our lives were calm, uneventful, almost boring at times after nine years in the military and living and working overseas. I was getting a little restless. Irene and I even discussed returning to our old life in the RAF. I even went so far as to find out how to go about it. It turned out that if I re-enlisted, it would be as a senior aircraftman (SAC), not a corporal. That would mean taking a big step back and lower pay. It had taken eight years to reach my previous level, and I did not fancy starting again. Irene seemed content enough. She always seemed to enjoy any job that she did, and she was always popular with her workmates, both female and male. She was a model employee, quick to learn, and conscientious.

We did all the usual things that people did in those days. Day trips in the car to Blackpool, which had not changed much since I went there with my grandma when I was just a kid. We bought our first television and spent the winter nights glued to the screen whilst huddling round the coal fire when the snow was on the ground and the windows were iced up.

In the end, the cold got to us. That year was the second coldest on record, and we craved sunshine and heat after being in the Mediterranean for three years. We looked into the places around the world that were available. I loved the couple of days I spent in Vancouver, Canada, but that was no place to get away from the cold. New Zealand was better but at the back of beyond.

That left Australia or South Africa. I got books from the local library on conditions in both countries, and it quickly become obvious that South Africa was undergoing big changes. Not all of them to the good. That left Australia. We wrote to Australia House in London, asking them for information and soon received leaflets and application forms that would enable us to apply for emigration. We liked what we saw of Australia, and after a short period of indecision, we threw caution to the wind and filled in the forms to emigrate to Australia ASAP.

CHAPTER 15

Australia Here we Come.

We left from Dover on the M. S. *Fairsky*. The first port of call was the Canary Islands and then on to Cape Town (the Suez Canal was closed at that time), where we were able to go ashore. We wandered about the docks area with the majestic Table Mountain as a backdrop and no real idea where we were. But it was good to get off the ship and stretch our legs. We left Cape Town on the tide and set off, with the next stop Perth in Western Australia.

Up to now the sea had been calm. But once out in the South Atlantic, all that changed as mighty rollers tossed the ship around like a toy. Marcelle and I were OK, but Irene and Nick were seasick, along with most of the other passengers. At mealtime, tables in the dining room were deserted except for the lucky few of us who were crafted by the rough seas. After a few days of this, crew members went from cabin to cabin with trays of food, trying to get people to eat something.

We finally arrived at Fremantle, the port for Perth. No sooner were we tied up dockside than scores of passengers we had not seen since Cape Town came tumbling down the gangplank. One or two were seen on their knees, kissing the ground.

The few passengers whose destination was Perth disembarked, and we were off again. I well remember the captain on the ship's Tannoy system warning us all that the Great Australian Bight was famous—or should that be infamous—for rough seas. There were groans from the newly rejuvenated passengers.

However, we were spared more rough seas, and the final journey to the port of Melbourne, Victoria, was calm. I think after about fifty of us left the ship, it went on to its destination of Sydney.

There were several coaches waiting for us at the docks, and as soon as we boarded and all our luggage was stowed, we were off to the railway station to catch the train to Adelaide. As we had sailed past Adelaide on our journey to Melbourne, I was a bit puzzled why we had not disembarked there. Nobody ever explained that to us. Perhaps the ship was too big for the Adelaide docks. The train left for Adelaide in the evening and was due to arrive next afternoon. We travelled sitting in the everyday carriages with no sleeping bunks. I thought that was a bit hard on the children, who were falling asleep sitting up, and we had not left Melbourne yet.

"You get what you pay for," as the old saying goes. I suppose an ocean voyage with all mod cons, followed by an overnight train was not bad value for £10. And that was just for the adults; the kids had just travelled thousands of miles for free! The train ride was uneventful. The children slept most of the way, stretched out on the seats. Irene and I managed a couple of hours, an end off. As it was night-time there was nothing to see to keep our interest.

Gradually, daylight filtered through the windows as we crossed the border into South Australia. At last we were able to get a good look at what was to be our new home. For a while, at least, it was the Pennington Migrant Hostel.

It reminded me of some of the military bases I lived in with corrugated iron huts and a dining hall. There was a sports field and a swing park for the children. The rule was we did not pay anything—no rent and no fees for food—until we were in paid employment. Priority number one was to get a job. And quickly!

As she always managed to do, Irene was the first to find employment. She went to work on the production line at a factory in Woodville, which was an adjoining suburb, and quite close to the hostel. It was a bit too far to walk, though, so we invested some of the cash that we had in a car, which would take Irene to work and me around the area seeking employment. I eventually got a job at the same company as Irene but in the office, where my keyboard skills learned in the air force proved very useful. We stayed in the hostel the best part of a year, long enough to find our way around the city and adjoining areas. We moved out of the hostel to the suburb of Semaphore, just one street back from the waterfront. With both of us working, we felt we could afford the rent, which was higher than average because of the location so close to the beach. The proximity to the beach was worth the extra rent as on the hot summer days and nights we often took a blanket each and slept there, along with dozens if not hundreds of others seeking a cool sea breeze on forty-degree days and close to thirty-degree nights.

I was always an avid reader, and the local newspaper, *The Advertiser*, was bought nearly every day. I always checked out the situations vacant page, and one day there was an advert for the post office. They were recruiting for the telegram department and holding an examination in a couple of weeks. There was a phone number, so I thought I would give it a try. I rang the number and put my name down. I later received a letter, telling me to report to the Adelaide University on Saturday morning on a date and time a couple of weeks away. There the examination would take place.

On the appointed day, I turned up on north terrace in the City Centre, expecting there would be a few of us. There were hundreds of people milling around and looking for parking spaces.

After walking around the building a few times, trying to find the right place to get in, I noticed a signboard with instructions signs and, "This way to the exam room," with arrows pointing down the corridor.

When I finally located the room, it was enormous, with dozens of desks. As I found out later, there was another room next door with dozens more desks. Somebody told me later there was more than two hundred people sitting the tests; I think that was probably a guess. There were three exams each, with a fifteen-minute break. The whole exercise lasted two and a half hours.

It was eventually revealed to me via a letter from the post office that my application had been successful, and I was to go to an address in the city, where I would officially join the post office and start a three-month training course. On the big day, I turned up to the address given. It was a quite small building, and I thought, You *could not get a lot of people in there.* I was right. There were five of us. It was apparently based on the scores from the test, and we had the five highest scores. I came third (apparently).

Three weeks later, I had resigned from my previous job and was about to start at the post office training section. I travelled into the city every day for that three-month period, I very soon realised that I could not take my car as the training building had no car park, and the prices to park every day for eight hours in the public car parks were out of the question.

The training course was really just a lesson of how to do things the post office way. There were typing tests, and general information on how to deal with the public.

At the end of the three months of training, we were introduced to the telegram office in the city, and after a couple days induction, we were on our own. One of the reasons for recruiting new staff was to fill three vacancies in Alice Springs.

They first asked for volunteers. One of the existing staff gave me the tip. He said, "If you don't want to go to Alice Springs, all <u>you</u> have to do is don't volunteer." As a married man with children, it would cost the post office a lot more than to send a single man. And as the other four successful recruits were all single, the odds were in my favour.

Irene and I talked about it, and we were eventually convinced that it would be great thing to do. After all, we came to Australia seeking adventure and a more active lifestyle. And we were sure that both of those things were more likely in the Northern Territory (NT) than in Adelaide. I volunteered to go. As there were three staff vacancies, two of my fellow trainees came with me.

At this time the railway to the NT only went as far as The Alice, and there was a narrow-gauge track from Port Augustan in South Australia, a few hours' drive to the north. So on the allotted day, Irene, the children, and I got on the train in Port Augusta, having driven there in our car. Behind the passenger carriages were several flatbed car carriers, so after the family was directed to their seats, I had to run the car up a ramp and on to the first flatbed, and drive it to the first empty car carrier.

The gap between each flatbed was covered by a couple of rickety boards, not much wider than the wheels on the car. I am not quite sure how, but I was able to succeed in getting to the first available flatbed without incident. I heaved a sigh of relief and joined the family in the passenger part of the train. The uppermost thought in my head was, *Will I have to reverse across those gaps when we reach our destination?*

Because of the narrow gauge, the train, known as the Ghan in memory of the Afghan camel drivers who used to carry goods through the trackless desert, the journey was extended as the top speed was only about 25 mph.

The countryside we crossed was arid and mostly treeless, flat for the most part but with outcrops of rock here and there. For hour after hour, there was no sign of human habitation. We were starting to wonder what we were getting ourselves into.

The McDonald Mountain Range came into view just in time to prevent major worry. They stretched from side to side of the horizon until, in the distance, the railway track seemed to vanish into a small hole in the mountain, Simpsons Gap. I had no idea who "Simpson" was, but the gap port enabled us to pull into the railway station of The Alice as the town was known to its residents.

My worry about having to reverse my car off the train was relieved when a motorised crane pulled alongside and expertly hooked the car off the flatbed and carefully placed it on the ground. I loved The Alice already.

The supervisor of the telegraph station (my boss) met us at the station and told us to follow him to our house. It was in a quiet cul-de-sac in the middle of town which went by the name of Knicker Place. He assured us it had nothing to do with underwear but was named after an early pioneer, Nurse Knicker, who was a heroine of the Alice Springs Hospital.

The house was a single-storey brick cottage with plenty of room. Though nothing fancy, it was adequately furnished, plain but serviceable. I was surprised to see there was a gas-fired heater in the main room. When winter came, we soon realised why it was needed as the nights were typical desert, and the water pipes froze several times during our time there. Our time in the NT had begun, which unfortunately meant another school for the kids. But to their great credit, they seemed to take it all in stride. I was put to work almost immediately as the person I was replacing had already left, and I never actually met him.

Like most outback towns, shortage of younger men was a big problem in The Alice, and I was soon involved in the football (soccer!) and squash racquets.

Irene, as she always did, got a part-time job with flexible hours working as a maid, cleaning and renewing bedclothes, changing sheets, and so on. She was able to see the children to school and to pick them up after. Even school holidays were not a problem as she simply took them to work with her. They spent time in the motel pool (they could swim) and helped with the cleaning.

I worked in the post office, and she worked in a motel on the edge of town, so we saw very little of each other during the day. In the evenings, we played squash, on different teams of course. We took trips to the drive-in cinema a couple times a week (no TV.). On weekends, it was football for me, and Nick played in the under tens competition.

Running through the centre of town was the River Todd, except there was no water in it. Until one day I was at work, and the boss came in and said he just had word from a friend who lived a few miles to the north. Due to the large amount of rain we had experienced lately, there was water in the river for the first time in years. The boss said it was a sight worth seeing, and he would hold the fort if I wanted to see it. The river was only a short distance away from the post office, so I agreed and ran down the street to the riverbank, where a crowd was already gathering as the word had gotten around. There was nothing to see yet, but there was a distant noise from upstream, which was getting louder by the minute. Then suddenly, with a roar, a wall of water two metres high came surging down the riverbed where five or so aboriginal children were standing. Too late they become aware of the danger they were in. And before anyone could react, the wall of water was upon them, bowling them over, and sweeping them down the river.

They could swim, but the sheer power of the initial wave was too strong. Among the crowd who had come to see the spectacle was a member of the local commonwealth police force. He was one of my football-playing friends.

Two of the bigger boys managed to swim and scramble on to the riverbank. But the others were in trouble. The policeman yelled to a couple of bystanders to give him a hand. Some of the nearest formed a human chain, linking hands with the police officer, who was in water up to his chest. He managed to grab one of the boys, who was passed back along the chain. They then ran down the riverbank and managed to rescue the rest of the children, bringing them to safety.

After being dry for years, the River Todd commenced to flow for nine months. Then one day, it was gone.

We had been in The Alice for a year, and I had two-week holiday coming up. We decided to drive down the road to what was then known as Ayers Rock—better known now us Uluru—a huge monolith to the south. It was a six-hour drive, and we in a two-car convoy with another friend and his family.

We had a break at a roadhouse on the Stuart Highway, where the entertainment consisted of a dingo "singing" accompanied by the owner of the roadhouse on his harmonica. There were twenty or so travellers there at the time, so when the hat was passed round, it was generously loaded with cash. A nice little earner and typical of the ingenuity of the outback, where anything could be made to earn its keep, even a wild dog!

Ayers Rock was impressive. It was visible from afar, and the closer we got, the more it dominated the landscape.

We were booked into the local motel, so we dropped our bags off and went to climb the rock and look at the view. We soon found out that rock climbing was frowned upon by the local people

We were told that from time to time, a climber would fall from a great height, often to his or her death. The locals regarded that as retribution for failing to do the right thing. And who could argue with that?

Instead we walked around the base of the rock, admiring the art work that was in every nook and cranny protected from the weather.

There were many overhangs and even some shallow caves to be explored. The days were interesting, but the nights were glorious, with a magnificent display of stars and a full moon that was surely larger than the regular moon!

CHAPTER 17

Return to The Alice

Time to load up the cars and be on our way. The journey back was mostly uneventful, except that the side road that led to the Stuart Highway was unpaved. Or in the local idiom, it was "a dirt road." We were only half an hour on our way, and the road was giving the car's suspension a real battering. And after hitting one sharp-edged piece of rock too many, we got a puncture in the left rear tyre. I managed to pull over to the side of the road on a level bit of desert.

Out with the spare and the jack. The problem was there was no firm ground on which to place the jack. I removed the damaged wheel and tried the spare. It was when I tried to jack up the car to fit the new wheel that it sank in the soft sand. So instead of the car going up, the jack was going down into the ground.

We looked around for a piece of rock or anything to stand the jack on to prevent it from sinking. But this was a desert road, and rock that big was in short supply. The sun was up, and it was getting hotter. We had to find a solution, and soon.

We searched in the boot of the car for something to act as a base, so I could get it light enough to get the wheel nuts on and tightened. The only solid thing in the boot was a petrol can, half full of petrol. It was metal, so if I could get it under the jack, it might just work.

I dug the sand away with my hands until I had a hole big enough to put the petrol can in. So far, so good. Luckily, before putting the almost-empty petrol can in the hole, I had filled it with sand, of which there was plenty. I quickly placed the spare on the axel and started to lower the car. As soon as I could, I put the wheel nuts on and screwed them tight. Seconds later, the steel jack pierced the petrol can, and the car dropped back to its rightful position, with four wheels on the road. As I said earlier, the rest of the trip was mostly uneventful!

CHAPTER 18

Decisions Decisions.

The end of my two-year posting was drawing ever closer with three choices looming. I could sign on here for another two years, or I could return to Adelaide. The third choice was to transfer to Darwin. Going back to Adelaide and commuting to the city every day did not appeal to either of us after the wide-open spaces of the NT. So that narrowed it down to two. Irene and I were happy in The Alice, and the children loved it. But it was a small town a thousand miles from anywhere and lacking some of the thing's city dwellers took for granted like television, and good medical facilities, restaurants, and theatres; there was a drive-in cinema. But basic facilities were the rule. We threw caution to the wind and opted to give Darwin a go.

The day before we left on the long drive up to Darwin, a letter was delivered by hand (no stamp or return address). It was a greeting card from somebody called Jan, wishing us all the best for the future. A handwritten note said something along the lines of, "Thanks for everything, and if you are ever in The Alice again, give me a call."

The name was unfamiliar, so I asked Irene who Jan was. She said it was one of the motel staff she had worked with, and they had become quite friendly. Jan was short for Janet or Jeanette, she wasn't sure.

I worked in the telegraph office. I sent and received telegrams all over the world, and it just so happened that a few days before, a telegram arrived in the office from the Netherlands for the manager of the motel who went by the name of Jan, which in that country was pronounced Yan, and it was a man's name! At least it gave me a reason to leave Alice Springs and never to mention that name again. I didn't make a fuss about it. What was the point?

The house in Darwin was a typical top-end building with the laundry and garage on the ground floor, and the living accommodations on the floor above. It was in the same street as the school, which was handy but well away from the city centre and shops.

It was immediately obvious that this city had no resemblance to any other place we had lived. The climate was unbearable in the wet season, hot and humid for five months of the year, and the time period known as "the build-up," which was the beginning of the wet season. When the storm clouds gathered with temperatures in the mid-thirties, rain threatened but seldom actually happened. Then one day, thunder and lightning banging and flashing, the rain came down in torrents. Early evening was the favoured time, and sitting on the veranda with the rain bucketing down around you is something I will never forget.

CHAPTER 19

Darwin For Better or For Worse.

When I told my boss in The Alice that I had volunteered for Darwin, he said, "You won't like it." He was right. It wasn't just the weather, which was awful for half the year. It is difficult to understand, but the place had an aura about it. Many of the people we knew there were sent to Darwin from Adelaide or the eastern states, and they could not wait to return to their state of origin. True, there were some long-term residents, but even they resented being sent there but had grown to like the place, almost against their wills. We were there, so we were determined to make the most of it and not join the ranks of the "whining poms."

One of our favourite places was the casino. It had several ways to part you from your money, but the one we liked the best was "2up," a traditional Aussie game where two coins were tossed in the air from a small wooden paddle, and bets were laid on whether they would land heads or tails. It was a simple but highly addictive way to separate punters from their money. There were also roulette wheels and, of course, the one-armed bandits—the fruit machines. We were careful not to go there too often as it was too easy to become addicted, and many people did.

I was still playing football, but my heart was not in it. It was hard to run around, chasing a football, when it was thirty-six degrees centigrade, and raining. We survived the wet season, and with the arrival of "the dry," we managed to get in some tennis and fishing, which was a little bit dangerous due to the presence in the waters around Darwin of crocodiles, big crocodiles.

Hit with the build- up imminent and the prospect of another wet, looming, our thoughts were turning to milder, cooler climes. The Darwin of the early seventies was instrumental in us leaving Australia all together. It is embarrassing to admit, but we were lured into becoming "ping-pong poms" and returning to Britain. Not just back to Britain but back to Oldham, the town of my and Irene's births.

We rented a second-floor, council-owned apartment, which was very modern with central heating and all mod cons. I got a job with the post office telegraph department. My experience with the Australian post office made for a smooth transition as the operating systems were very similar. The department that I was employed in was in the heart of the centre business district in Manchester. With a bus to the city every twenty-five minutes, or a twenty-minute car journey, being in the main city meant it was uneconomical to use the car to get to work because of the parking fees.

On one of the rare occasions that I took the car to work, I parked on a bit of spare ground in a back alley off the main street. And, of course, it was stolen, I reported it to the local police station. After a few weeks, it was located, abandoned in a remote car park on the edge of the city, undamaged. The police thought it likely someone used it to get home from the city after a night out. I was glad to see it and only parked in secure areas in the future.

I played football in the Manchester Wednesday league; Wednesday was early-closing day. It was very competitive, but we had a secret weapon; four of our team were Catholic priests. So we must have had some help from above. The last game of the season was between us and a team of Manchester taxi drivers, winner take all. The teams were evenly matched. The last time we played them was a one-all.

But this time it was on our own ground. We won the game one goal to nil. One of the priests' scored the goal.

CHAPTER 20

Second Thoughts.

It was 1974, and the bug was biting again. It wasn't discussed, but privately, Irene and I wondered if we had been a little hasty in scuttling back to Britain. Surely there were lots of places in Australia that would have been better destinations. It had only taken one northern winter to point this out, and with another freezing-cold winter looming, thoughts of Adelaide crept in. Returning to Australia would break my mother's heart and lead to yet another change of school for the children, but it was becoming obvious that we had overreacted to Darwin and conveniently forgotten why we left Britain in the first place. We did not have enough money for all of us to travel together, so it was decided that I would go alone. The rest of the family would follow as soon as we could raise the fare. We gave up the apartment, and Irene and the children moved in with my sister, Pam, until I could raise the funds.

I was met at the airport in Adelaide by my good friend Jim, who insisted that I stay with him and his family until I could get enough funds to reunite the family.

Jim and Marlene lived in the northern part of the city, in Elizabeth, a new and expanding residential area. I was able to find employment at the Holden Car Manufacturing Company who paid good money and were always hiring new staff.

I can never thank Jim and Marlene enough. They treated me like one of the family and refused my offer to pay my share of the costs. They said that way I would be able to raise the funds for the family to join us much quicker. In the end, it took about four months to raise the money and reunite the family. All I can say is that without the help and support of Jim and Marlene, it would have been a lot longer. In the years to come, I was able to help Jim in a similar way, much to my delight.

We rented a house one street back from the Salisbury Highway, and Jim again came to our rescue. An American chewing gum company was establishing itself in Australia. Jim had been hired and was asked if he knew any suitable person who could do the job. To his credit, he nominated me. It paid more than the job at Holden, and it came with a car supplied. The company was starting from scratch, so the work consisted of persuading the owners of sweets and confectionary stores to give our product a try.

Another man recruited to do the job was a Scotsman, so with Jim being Irish, we had the perfect credentials for all the Englishman, Irishman, and a Scotsman jokes. But the work itself was no joke. We travelled all over the state and even up into the NT and northwest to Broken Hill, so it involved a lot of driving. But the product sold itself. It was advertised widely, on television and in newspapers and magazines. It was almost just a case of doing the rounds and taking orders. It was all rather routine and monotonous, and except for the long-distance driving, not very challenging.

One day there was an ad in the *Advertiser*, the local Adelaide paper. The Civil Aviation Authority was advertising for aeronautical telecommunications officers (ATOs). I liked the sound of that, so I applied. I attended an interview in the city, and within a short time, I received a letter informing me that I had been successful, subject to a medical, which was arranged in Adelaide the following week. I duly attended and was given a clean bill of health. I was in. The next step was to attend a five-month training course in Melbourne. Fortunately, Irene had passed her driving test some time before, so there were no problems getting to work whilst I was away. We had recently bought a house in the Adelaide Houghton suburb of Ingle Farm, which had a high school for Marcelle, who was twelve. Nick, however, chose to stay at his present school in Salisbury as he only had a year left to do. Also, I think he had enough changing of schools in his fifteen years of life. It meant a tricky bike ride every day, but when he turned sixteen, he would be able to get a motorbike or even a car.

Irene, as she always did, landed a good job in Elizabeth, working for Levi's jeans manufacturers. It was about a thirty-minute drive.

CHAPTER 21

It was an easy drive to Melbourne via Mount Gambier and the Great Ocean Road. It was very scenic in places and new territory for me. The recruiting drive for ATOs had been Australia-wide, so the class was comprised of men and women from all mainland states except WA. We were all accommodated in motels except, of course, for Melbourne residents. There were sixteen of us in all, and we were a diverse and lively bunch.

We travelled into the city by tram mostly. In fact, my car was in the motel car park for so long it was reported to the authorities as abandoned, possibly stolen. To avoid further dramas of this kind, I made sure I went for a short drive somewhere, anywhere! The course itself was similar in many ways to things I was taught when I was in the RAF. The main difference being instead of bomber command, I would be dealing with Qantas and other national and international airlines. One of the highlights of the course was a flight to Tasmania and back in a twin-engine, prop-driven aircraft owned by the Department of Civil Aviation, presumably to give us an insight into what our new jobs would be involved in. Not that any flying would be involved, more like making the flights of others safer and more comfortable.

CHAPTER 22

More Training – Melbourne.

Back in Adelaide, the family was getting along fine in my absence. The schools were on holiday, and Marcelle was about to come to Melbourne for a holiday. Unfortunately, she was not allowed to stay with me as the DCA was footing the bill for that. But my sister, Pam, was living in Melbourne at that time, so she could stay with her.

The course finally came to an end, and we celebrated with dinner at a local bar. Irene came over from Adelaide, which was a joyful reunion after five months apart. The bar was in the town of Saint Kilda and had been our "local" during our stay. There was 100 percent turnout for the dinner and a festive air to the evening as everyone except two of class graduated. Even the two who didn't were offered slightly lesser jobs with the department, with the added attraction that they could be upgraded in the future, subject to a short course of in-house training.

The end of the course's big night out was a great success, culminating by Irene getting the biggest laugh of the evening. True to her usual lack of control when under the influence of no more than two glasses of wine, she first missed her chair when sitting down after a toast to our instructors, who were, of course, invited. She missed the chair by a good margin and landed bottom down on the floor, which brought a round of applause from the assembly. It is a good thing that she is so small in stature, as I had to practically carry her back to the motel.

We left Melbourne to return to Adelaide the next day. We drove back via the Great Ocean Road, a truly magnificent feast of cliffs and ocean, and miles of deserted and lonely beaches. Just Irene and I, as Marcelle had returned in time for the new term at school.

The first day at Adelaide Airport consisted mainly of being shown around and introduced to my fellow workers. Our situation in the building was in the briefing office, where the pilots came to file their flight plans and get their weather reports and forecasts. It was interesting and responsible work, and I was looked forward to getting involved. I was an ATO, certainly the longest title of any job I have ever had before or since. Years later, it was shortened to aeronautical data systems officer, which was not much of an improvement when filling in the name and occupation column on my tax return.

On the July 19, 1976, we became Australian citizens and took the Oath of Allegiance. The ceremony was performed in the city of Salisbury, north of Adelaide. We saw as an act of some significance, but I still had a soft spot for England when it came to cricket and "the ashes."

In order to qualify for promotion, I studied at night school for two years, taking two subjects a year. I qualified for the University of Adelaide adult matriculation certificate on January 14, 1980.

It was about this time that the family started to take an interest in horses. There were fields and stables just down the road from our house, and Irene and Marcelle had a couple of horses that were treated more like pets than working or show horses. But it was a relaxing hobby they both enjoyed together, and they spent hours looking after them.

CHAPTER 23

Health Problems

Irene had read somewhere that long-term use of the contraceptive pill was the cause of some female ailments in later life. She had been using the pill ever since her miscarriage back in Cyprus and felt she should examine some alternatives. After consulting her doctor and some of her workmates who had tubal ligations, she thought that was the best way to go.

It consisted of surgery whereby the "tubes" in her lower abdomen were cut and tied, so she would no longer be able to conceive. She consulted a specialist, and an appointment was made. On the appointed day, we drove to the doctor's surgery in North Adelaide. The operation was scheduled for no longer than thirty minutes or so, followed by a couple of hours rest and recuperation, so I elected to stay in the doctor's waiting room and then with her until she was OK to travel. When she was taken into surgery, I settled down to read a magazine.

After about forty minutes, the receptionist called me into a small ward with a couple of beds in it. Irene was tucked up in one of them. I was told that all had gone well, and Irene needed a period of rest. The surgeon would look in on her in an hour or so to make sure she was fit to travel, and if so, we could go home. With a cry of, "Call me if you need me," she left us alone. Irene was alert but looked a little tired. But she said she felt OK. After about ten minutes, she said she felt like she was losing blood from the operation site. She asked me if I could have a look and check. I pulled back the bedsheet, and there was blood everywhere. The whole of the top half of the bed was soaked, and it was spreading even as I looked at it. I quickly covered it up again; I did not want her to see it. I ran down the corridor to get the doctor, who was in the front office, talking to the receptionist. I grabbed him by the arm and yelled, "Come quick! She is bleeding badly." To his credit, he ran hard back to the ward, threw back the cover, and took a step back. She was still haemorrhaging still. A trolley was quickly brought in, and Irene was put on it and taken back to the theatre. After about twenty minutes, the nurse came back to me and told me the doctor had managed to stem the blood flow and was currently adding extra stitches. She assured me that Irene was out of danger, but because of the recent events, they wanted to keep her overnight to make absolutely sure all was well. I gave her my phone number, and she said they would call me tomorrow, and all being well, I could take her home then.

I was on the afternoon shift the next day, starting work at noon. When I had not heard from the clinic by eleven, I was forced to call work and tell them I would not be coming in as I had an emergency to deal with at home (known in Australia as a sickie). This meant that somebody on a day off would have to be called in to take my place as the position had to be occupied 24/7. It was close to four o'clock before I finally got the phone call telling me to come and pick her up. She was a bit shaky still but soon seated in the car. I asked the doctor if she needed any medication or special treatment, but he thought not, just rest and not to do anything that involved heavy lifting, such as moving furniture or gardening.

The last thing he said before we left was right out of left field. He took me by the arm and whispered in my ear, "You'll be OK. I put a tuck in it for you." Not very professional of him but as it turned out, true!

Irene's recuperation was going well. She took a few days off work but insisted she was well enough to work on the coming Monday. Her job was one where she sat most of the time, so it was OK for her to return to it.

Nick was seeing a girl who lived "down south," Mclaren Vale. He did some work for her father during the long school holiday, which enabled him to buy a car. So it was goodbye to the bicycle. He took his driving test and passed, which meant he was much more mobile and could get to school and down to his girl friend's at the weekend. He left school at sixteen and started work at the factory of Levi Strauss, making jeans. Just like his mum.

CHAPTER 24

Houghton

The horses began to take up more of Irene's and Marcelle's time. We began thinking of moving to the near country, somewhere with a bit of land, where we could expand the number of horses and maybe do some more competitive riding rather than just hobby riding. Meanwhile, Marcelle had recently met a young man from Elizabeth, who was also interested in the idea. We started to look at the land for sale in the inner areas as Irene and I still had to go to work, and we did not want too long a drive every day.

After months of searching and many drives in the near countryside, we came on a property of twenty-six acres and only ten minutes from the local shopping centre. Besides the land, there was a house with adequate accommodations. Several outbuildings, including a barn, and importantly, stables were also included. It was just what we were looking for. We snapped it up and moved in after a few weeks.

In addition to the land, there was a spring that supplied water for the horses. There was the basics of a garden in front of the house, which was situated on top of a high ridge, giving us a fine view along the valley. We had everything we needed. Glen, Marcelle's boyfriend, had already entered competitive events with one of the horses and done very well. With the purchase of an Appaloosa mare, we hoped to raise the bar a little.

By this time, Nick was working in Salisbury for an iconic Australian company and appeared settled with a new partner after he and his first partner separated. He was still living with us at Houghton at this time, enjoying the freedom and fresh air like the rest of us. Eventually, he moved in with her. The main event of this time was Marcelle and Glens wedding, which went off without a hitch. They have gone on through thick and thin to this day.

Glen competed successfully on many occasions with one or the other Appaloosas, even going to Victoria and winning trophies.

It was high summer, with temperatures in the forties. One afternoon I was at work when one of the office guys received notification of a bushfire in our part of the Adelaide hills. One of the air traffic controllers tuned in his radio to find out more. The next thing we heard, the fire was in the vicinity of the village of Houghton, I contacted my boss and told him what was happening. He offered to sit in for me if I wanted to go as it might become necessary to evacuate the livestock. So it was into the car and head for home. As I got to the point of the road where the main road splits into two, there was a police roadblock on the main road. Even though I showed them my address on my licence, they would not let me through. The secondary road wandered around the hill a bit, but I thought I could still use it to get home. By this time, there were great plumes of smoke rising from the wooded slopes ahead of me. I eventually came to a road that was burnt out but passable, with burnt trees on both sides of the road. But so far, no actual flames.

I came to the junction leading to my home, and it was clear, no roadblock or police. I quickly headed down the left lane leading up the valley and up to my parking spot. There was smoke coming from the top of the bank, but the fire had not yet crossed the road to our property. The fire brigade was there in numbers and seemed to be holding the line to the other road that crossed to the right of our land.

Ultimately, the fire brigade stopped the blaze at the tarmac road that was the boundary to our property. As the rest of the family returned from their various workplaces, we walked around to see just how close a shave it had been.

After the fire, it was never the same. What had always seemed a haven was shown to be the opposite. In that wooded part of the area, there could be another fire any time of day or night. It was time for a rethink. In reality, the property we had was too big for the use we were putting it to. Though most of the land was not utilised, it still had to be managed but with no return for our efforts.

Inevitably, we were looking to move—again. We advertised the property for sale, and there was immediate interest. We eventually sold it to a young, single man, who had a big win on the lottery, so the sale went through quickly.

Irene and I had looked at a house for sale in the northern suburb of <u>Para Hills</u>. It seemed to cater to our needs. And it was affordable and ready to move in. It was also much closer to our various workplaces, cutting the commute time for me by a good twenty minutes. In fact, it is the next suburb to Ingle Farm, so in a way, it was like coming home.

CHAPTER 25

The house at Para Hills was about halfway up the hill. It had views across the valley to the second airport at Parafield, where I was occasionally sent to work. It was only used by light aircraft but was busy with take-offs and landings all day. My travel time to work was about three minutes. We soon settled in our new home. We spent less time getting to and from work, and not having to worry about the threat of bushfires was a great relief. But as often the case, we were soon provided with something else to worry about. I was on a day off from work, and Irene arrived home early. She had become unwell, and her supervisor told her to go home. I made her an appointment with the doctor, who examined her and said it seemed she had a heart attack. She was to see a specialist as soon as possible. The thought came to me that she had driven home with a dodgy heart!

After an expert examination, it was confirmed that her heart was damaged. The doctor recommended a heart bypass as soon as it could be arranged. Admission to the Royal Adelaide Hospital on North Terrace was organised, and a date was set. On the appointed day, we arrived at the hospital to find that when the patients were being admitted, the next of kin, of which there were about ten, were to attend a graphic film about the operation (not the same one Irene was having) in order to demonstrate what our loved ones were about to go through. It is a good thing that the film was only shown to the next of kin because if they had let the patients see what they were about to have done to them, well, the word "graphic," hardly does it justice. They would have run from the hospital, never to return.

Irene survived the operation and was in the recovery ward, sleeping. I crept quietly in and sat by her bed. She heard me come in and stirred. She seemed to be waving her hand at me, but then I realised that it was two fingers to her lips. I could hardly believe it; she wanted a cigarette! I think it was a no smoking hospital, so I could not have given her one even if I wanted to, which I most certainly did not.

During the operation, a vein or artery was taken from the thigh and used in the heart. Irene had no end of trouble with this. After having open-heart surgery, she had to go to another part of the hospital to have the wound in her leg attended to. That leg was never the same again and was still sensitive to touch many years later. The rest of her recovered well. She was given a list of dos and don'ts (one of the latter was smoking) and told to rest and avoid anything strenuous for at least three months. We heard on the grapevine that of the group Irene was a part of, two patients had not survived. One was having the operation for the second time, which would become significant in years to come.

CHAPTER 26

We spent happy years at Para Hills, so we were not too happy when I was told there was a vacancy in Darwin, and my name was in the running for a transfer. Unlike the post office, you didn't get to choose; you were told that you were going. However, it was a two-year posting and then return to Adelaide, so there was no need to sell the house. Nick and his partner were currently renting, so it was arranged for them to live there for the two years, rent-free, thus enabling them to save a deposit to buy a home of their own. Once again, this time reluctantly, we headed for Darwin. But this time we were older, and I like to think wiser! We were given a two-storey house similar to the one the post office gave us years ago. But the furniture and fittings were superior, as was the location. And there were no schools to worry about this time.

We were also better prepared to deal with the wet and the humidity—still no air-conditioning. We knew a few people as well as they were ex-Adelaide Airport employees We quickly settled into the routine. And surprise, surprise, Irene got a job almost immediately at the local supermarket, where she rose through the ranks to the dizzy height of assistant supervisor with four underlings, all male.

I decided to give the soccer another go but dumped the squash racquets in favour of tennis with a fellow worker and his wife. He had been transferred three years ago and became so acclimatised he didn't want to leave.

Not much had changed in Darwin in the years we were absent. It was bigger, with more facilities, supermarkets, and the like. But there was the weather and the wet, and not much could be done about that.

That first Christmas, first Marcelle and her daughter, followed by Glen, came up and spent some time with us, which was great. Having a baby around the place made Irene's day.

One of Irene's fellow workers was getting married, and we were invited to the wedding. We were not sure of the protocol as the bride and groom were immigrants from India. We were told no gifts were required, just to bring ourselves.

So we did.

I had never seen so much food outside a supermarket. Every relative of the bride and groom—and there were dozens of them—brought bowls and dishes of food. Soon the huge table in the hall was overflowing, and the staff were hastily erecting collapsible tables to hold the excess. We did not understand a word of the ceremony, but everyone else did, and it was much appreciated by everyone. Oh, and all the food was eaten, every scrap.

Darwin had been mostly demolished by Cyclone Tracy in 1974, and some of the hasty rebuilding was not the prettiest urban areas around. But the casino was still there, as were the pool and the airport, of course, and we were better prepared this time. There were no children to worry about as our children had children of their own to worry about. Marcelle had a little girl, Jessica, and Nick had a boy named Sean after actor Sean Connery of James Bond fame.

We had another visit from Marcelle's family the second Christmas. Jess was eighteen months old and running around.

Our time in Darwin was nearly up, and we were looking forward to reuniting with the family. Nick and his partner went off to live with a relative of hers, and Marcelle and her family came to live in Para Hills with us. We had done our two years of penance in Darwin, and our reward was to unite our family once again in Adelaide

In 1994, Nicholas was killed in a road accident on his way to our house at Kalbeeba north of Gawler. The death certificate states the cause of death as haemorrhage due to fracture of the skull base.

Irene passed away on November 1, 1995, from cardiac failure. She had been admitted to the Modbury Hospital the day before. The first of November is my birthday, and during our life together, Irene never failed to send me a birthday card. This one was no exception. On returning home after she died, I went to make myself a cup of coffee. I opened the cupboard door, and a birthday card fell into my lap. She even sent me a card after she died!